To Dennis, Nancy, Liberty and Phoebe – K.G.
For Jessica and Emily – N.S.

You Do!
A RED FOX BOOK 0 09 943873 9

First published in Great Britain by The Bodley Head,
an imprint of Random House Children's Books

The Bodley Head edition published 2003
Red Fox edition published 2004

3 5 7 9 10 8 6 4 2

Red Fox Books are published by Random House Children's Books,
61–63 Uxbridge Road, London W5 5SA,
a division of The Random House Group Ltd,
in Australia by Random House Australia (Pty) Ltd,
20 Alfred Street, Milsons Point, Sydney, NSW 2061, Australia,
in New Zealand by Random House New Zealand Ltd,
18 Poland Road, Glenfield, Auckland 10, New Zealand,
and in South Africa by Random House (Pty) Ltd,
Endulini, 5A Jubilee Road, Parktown 2193, South Africa

THE RANDOM HOUSE GROUP Limited Reg. No. 954009

www.kidsatrandomhouse.co.uk

A CIP catalogue record for this book is available from the British Library.

Printed and bound in Singapore

You Do!

Kes Gray & Nick Sharratt

RED FOX

"Don't pick your nose,"
said Daisy's *mum.*
"You do," said Daisy.
"When?" said Daisy's *mum.*
"In the car on the way
to Nanny's," said Daisy.
"I wasn't picking,
I was scratching,"
explained Daisy's *mum.*

"Don't slurp your soup," said Daisy's *mum*.

"You do," said Daisy.

"When?" said Daisy's *mum*.

"On Saturday when we had chicken noodle," said Daisy.

"That's because I'd been to the dentist,"
explained Daisy's *mum*.

"Don't leave your clothes on the floor,"
said Daisy's *mum*.
"You do," said Daisy.
"When?" said Daisy's *mum*.
"Last week when you were going
to that party," said Daisy.
"I couldn't decide what to wear,"
explained Daisy's *mum*.

"Don't wear your wellies in the house," said Daisy's *mum.*

"You do," said Daisy.

"When?" said Daisy's *mum.*

"Last weekend when you came in from the garden," said Daisy.

"That's because I had to fill the watering can," explained Daisy's *mum.*

"Don't keep fidgeting," said Daisy's *mum*.

"You do," said Daisy.

"When?" said Daisy's *mum*.

"In the church at that wedding we went to," said Daisy.

"That's because the seats were too hard," explained Daisy's *mum*.

"Don't sit so close to the telly," said Daisy's *mum.*

"You do," said Daisy.

"When?" said Daisy's *mum.*

"When *you* were watching that soppy film," said Daisy. "I didn't have *my* contact lenses in," explained Daisy's *mum.*

"Don't talk with your mouth full," said Daisy's mum.

"You do," said Daisy.

"When?" said Daisy's mum.

"When your jacket potato was too hot," said Daisy.

"I wasn't talking, I was blowing,"
explained Daisy's mum.

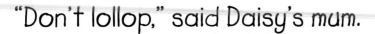

"Don't lollop," said Daisy's mum.

"You do," said Daisy.

"When?" said Daisy's mum.

"Last Monday evening," said Daisy.

"I'd just done my exercises,"

explained Daisy's mum.

"Don't eat all the nice ones," said Daisy's *mum*.

"You do," said Daisy.

"When?" said Daisy's *mum*.

"All the time," said Daisy.

"That's because I only like the nice ones,"
explained Daisy's *mum*.

"Don't keep saying **'you do'**,"
said Daisy's *mum*.

"You do," chuckled Daisy.

Daisy's *mum* put her hands on her hips and looked Daisy straight in the eye.
"I do not keep saying 'you do', **YOU DO!**"

"You just said it **TWICE!**" giggled Daisy.

"Right, who deserves a good tickling?" laughed Daisy's *mum*, chasing Daisy into the garden.

"I DO! I DO!"
squealed Daisy.

Find out more about Daisy!

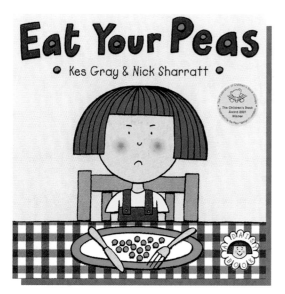

✿ Mum tries everything to get Daisy to eat her peas. But does she eat them, or will she turn the tables on Mum?

Winner of the Children's Book Award,
Stockport Schools Book Award for KS1,
Sheffield Children's Book Award, and
Experian Big 3 Award
Shortlisted for the Blue Peter Award

✿ Daisy has never had a babysitter before.
Will Angela be fooled by all her fibs?
And will Daisy really, really get away with it?

✿ Daisy is a bridesmaid at Auntie Sue's wedding, but Daisy doesn't do dresses and she certainly doesn't do lovely. What *will* Daisy wear?

Come and play with Daisy at www.**kidsatrandomhouse**.co.uk/daisy